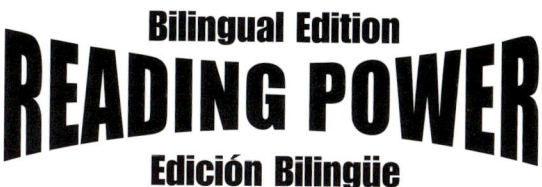

School Activities

Chorus

Coro

Rae Emmer

The Rosen Publishing Group's
PowerKids Press™ & Buenas Letras™
New York

Published in 2003 by The Rosen Publishing Group, Inc.
29 East 21st Street, New York, NY 10010
Copyright © 2003 by The Rosen Publishing Group, Inc.

All rights reserved. No part of this book may be reproduced in any form without permission in writing from the publisher, except by a reviewer.

First Bilingual Edition 2003
First Edition in English 2002

Book Design: Victoria Johnson
Photo Credits: Maura Boruchow

Thanks to Westtown School
Gracias a la Escuela Westtown

Emmer, Rae
Chorus/Coro/Rae Emmer ; traducción al español: Spanish Educational Publishing
p. cm. — (School Activities)
Includes bibliographical references and index.
ISBN 0-8239-6903-7 (lib. bdg.)
1. Choirs (Music)—Juvenile literature. [1. Choirs (Music) 2. Spanish Language Materials—Bilingual.] I. Title. II. School activities (New York, N.Y.)

Printed in The United States of America

Contents

Chorus	4
Learning New Songs	10
The Concert	16
Glossary	22
Resources	23
Index	24

Contenido

El coro	4
Nuevas canciones	10
El concierto	16
Glosario	22
Recursos	23
Índice	24

We have a chorus in school.

En la escuela
tenemos un coro.

There are many students in the chorus. We like to sing together.

El coro tiene muchos estudiantes.
Nos gusta cantar juntos.

We meet after school
to practice.

———————

Practicamos después de clases.

The teacher gives us new songs to sing.

La maestra nos da nuevas canciones.

We learn the words
we will sing.

Estudiamos la letra
de las canciones.

The teacher plays the songs on the piano. We sing along.

La maestra toca el piano.
Nosotros cantamos.

Tonight is the concert. We get ready. We must look our best.

Esta noche es el concierto.
Nos preparamos para cantar.
Tenemos que vernos bien.

We are on the stage. We are ready to sing.

———————

Estamos en el escenario. Estamos listos para cantar.

Our families enjoy the concert.

A nuestras familias
les gusta mucho el concierto.

Glossary

chorus (**kor**-uhs) a group of people who sing together

concert (**kon**-suhrt) a musical performance

piano (pea-**an**-oh) a large musical instrument with a keyboard and strings

practice (**prak**-tihs) to do something again and again to learn to do it well

stage (**stayj**) a place to put on shows

Glosario

concierto (el) actuación musical

coro (el) grupo de personas que cantan juntas

escenario (el) lugar donde se representa un espectáculo

piano (el) instrumento musical grande que tiene teclado y cuerdas

practicar hacer algo una y otra vez para aprender a hacerlo bien

Resources / Recursos

Here are more books to read about the chorus:
Otros libros que puedes leer sobre el coro:

Gonna Sing My Head Off!: American Folk Songs for Children
by Kathleen Krull
Alfred A. Knopf Books for Young Readers (1995)

Kids' Broadway Songbook: Songs Originally Sung Onstage by Children
Hal Leonard Corporation (Editor)
Hal Leonard Publishing (1995)

Web sites
Due to the changing nature of Internet links, PowerKids Press has developed an online list of Web sites related to the subject of this book. This site is updated regularly. Please use this link to access the list:

Sitios web
Debido a las constantes modificaciones en los sitios de Internet, PowerKids Press ha desarrollado una guía on-line de sitios relacionados al tema de este libro. Nuestro sitio web se actualiza constantemente. Por favor utiliza la siguiente dirección para consultar la lista:

http://www.buenasletraslinks.com/chl/tmb

Word count in English: 77
Número de palabras en español: 67

Index

C
chorus, 4, 6
concert, 16, 20

F
families, 20

P
piano, 14
practice, 8

S
school, 4, 8
songs, 10, 14
stage, 18
students, 6

T
teacher, 10, 14

W
words, 12

Índice

C
canciones, 10
concierto, 16, 20
coro, 4, 7

E
escenario, 18
escuela, 4
estudiantes, 7

F
familias, 20

L
letra, 12

M
maestra, 10, 15

P
piano, 15
practicar, 8